For Bob, who loved Ruth —K.K.Y.

To my family and Aaron, with love —S.K.

Hmong is pronounced MOHNG. The word refers to a people, an ethnic minority, from Southeast Asia. Starting in 1975, many Hmong families came to the United States as refugees of war.
Paj Ntaub is pronounced BA NDAO. The word refers to traditional needlework techniques used on items such as story cloths, which visually represent and document the experiences of the Hmong people across time, including families' journeys as refugees. It is also a girl's name.
Tais Tais is pronounced TIE TIE. The word refers to the maternal grandmother (the mother's mother).

Carolrhoda Books®
An imprint of Lerner Publishing Group, Inc.
241 First Avenue North
Minneapolis, MN 55401 USA

For reading levels and more information, look up this title at www.lernerbooks.com.

Designed by Emily Harris.
Main body text set in Janson Text LT Std.
Typeface provided by Adobe.
The illustrations in this book were created digitally using digital graphite, pastels, watercolor, and scanned handmade textures.

Library of Congress Cataloging-in-Publication Data

Names: Yang, Kao Kalia, 1980– author. | Kim, Seo (Illustrator), illustrator.
Title: A map into the world / Kao Kalia Yang ; illustrated by Seo Kim.
Description: Minneapolis : Carolrhoda Books, [2019] | Summary: Paj Ntaub, a young Hmong American girl, spends a busy year with her family in their new home and seeks a way to share the beauty of the world with a grieving neighbor.
Identifiers: LCCN 2018038403 (print) | LCCN 2018043257 (ebook) | ISBN 9781541561045 (eb pdf) | ISBN 9781541538368 (lb : alk. paper)
Subjects: | CYAC: Family life—Fiction. | Neighbors—Fiction. | Hmong Americans—Fiction. | Grief—Fiction.
Classification: LCC PZ7.1.Y3648 (ebook) | LCC PZ7.1.Y3648 Map 2019 (print) | DDC [E]—dc23

LC record available at https://lccn.loc.gov/2018038403

Manufactured in the United States of America
1-45000-35836-2/13/2019

A MAP INTO THE WORLD

KAO KALIA YANG
ILLUSTRATED BY SEO KIM

Carolrhoda Books • Minneapolis

The first time we saw the swing and the slide and the garden of the green house with the big windows, my mother sat down in a chair in the backyard and said she did not want to get up. Tais Tais and I looked at the garden, and she pointed out tomatoes, green beans, and a watermelon round as my mother's belly.

Tais Tais knelt down to touch the dirt.

I asked my mother if I could try the swing, and she said, “Yes, Paj Ntaub.”

The green house became our house. I helped Tais Tais hang the special story cloth about how the Hmong got to America on the empty wall by the big window of the living room.

We saw an old man and woman through the window. They waved. We waved back.

Later, my mother and father brought me across the street. The old man's name was Bob, and the old woman's name was Ruth. Up close, I could see that they were even older than Tais Tais.

Tais Tais and I were in the garden picking tomatoes and beans and checking on the watermelon when my parents brought my baby brothers home from the hospital. I ran to the gate. The boys were smaller than my baby dolls but cuter than any doll with their fuzzy heads and red lips and round brown eyes.

Some days the babies cried very loud. I covered my ears with my hands and asked my father to take me outside. Bob and Ruth sat on their special bench. We waved back and forth.

The leaves of the two gingko trees by Bob and Ruth's house turned yellow like apricots.

One day, a brisk wind blew and the fan-shaped leaves came flying down. They covered the grass and the street and the dark mouth of the drain. Bob raked while Ruth sat and watched.

I brought in a leaf for the babies to touch, but my mother said, "They're still too little, Paj Ntaub."

The snow made the world quiet around us. We stopped seeing Bob and Ruth outside. The snowflakes fell on their driveway and glittered in the gray light.

I made a ball of snow for my brothers, but it melted before they woke up from their nap.

At night, I looked out our big window at Bob and Ruth's house to see their lights shining across the dark street. Sometimes I saw a shape of a person looking back at me. I waved, but the shadow person never waved back.

On a cold morning, cars came to our block, filling the street. Car doors slammed as men and women in thick jackets walked quickly to Bob and Ruth's house.

My father said, "Ruth has died. Her family is coming to say goodbye."

I felt sad for Ruth. My brothers just
played with the toys above them.

The cars kept coming and
going the next day and the next.
I swayed back and forth on my
toes by the big window.

I tried to lift one of my brothers so the people could see how cute he was, but he cried and my mother said, "You're still too little to carry him, Paj Ntaub."

After the Hmong New Year, my baby brothers learned how to sit on their own and we all sat looking out the window together. I clapped for them when a plane flew across the high skies. They laughed every time.

The house across the street looked empty. The gingko trees reached for the sky with their thin fingers.

When the snow started melting, I could not wait to return to the swing and the slide and the garden. My baby brothers crawled all over the floor, underneath the table and the chairs. They were like puppies, their tongues licking everything.

I found the first worm of spring on the sidewalk and named her Annette. I wanted to bring her inside so my brothers could watch her wiggle, but my mother said, “I don’t think so, Paj Ntaub.”

The world became green again, and finally, we all went outside. Tais Tais planted green onions. I picked flowers from the lilac bushes for my brothers to smell.

They opened their mouths and tried to eat them. My mother said, "Don't let them eat the flowers, Paj Ntaub."

We took the babies outside again the next day after lunch. Bob's garage door opened, and we all watched as he pushed out his special bench. He sat down alone.

I pulled on my mother's sleeve until she looked at me. I whispered an idea in her ear.

My mother and I crossed the street and walked over to Bob. I let the sidewalk chalk bucket swing in my hands.

I asked my mother to ask Bob
if I could draw on his driveway.

I said, "If he doesn't like it, the rain
will come and wash it away."

Bob nodded and said, "Go ahead."

My mother and Bob talked in low voices. I could hear Bob say, "Ruth, she was with me for sixty years . . ."

I started my picture with a teardrop.

And then I made it splatter like sunshine.
I drew lines leading away from the
splattered sun in many directions . . .

I drew a line that led to the garden.
There, I put a yellow gingko leaf.

I drew a line that led to the grass.
There, I made the sparkling snow.

I drew a line to the sidewalk. There, I put a smiling worm named Annette.

I drew an arrow to our house. There, I added lilac flowers.

And then I drew a line, the biggest line of all, toward the street, and there I drew the whole world.

When I was done, I walked quietly to my mother and to Bob. They stopped talking, and Bob shook my hand.

"What did you draw for me?" he asked.

I said in a whisper, "A map into the world. Just in case you need it."

Bob said, “I think I might.”